ALI MAY

GEOGRAPHY OF ATTRACTION

MAYHART BOOKS

www.ali-may.com
info@ali-may.com

First published in Great Britain by Mayhart Books

Edited by Wallis Darke

Cover design by Elena Carl – www.elenacarl.de

Printed in England by Clays Ltd, St Ives plc.

A CIP catalogue record for this book is available
from the British Library

Paperback ISBN 978-0-9932453-0-5

STORIES

When it gets hot in Tehran

The first time I had sex was on a bus. It was when streets were narrower in Tehran but summers just as hot. City buses were imported second-hand from Germany and Hungary. Their interiors were refurbished to last a little longer; but the new seats, made of metal frames and foam cushions covered with cheap, faux leather, were not strong enough to tolerate vandalism of everyday. The seats were red or blue or green, but the colour didn't make much difference in giving passengers a pleasant experience. They were so worn you could feel the frames underneath. The covers were either jammed to granite hardness with overstuffing, or so yielding that the existence of the cushion over the frame was a moot point in terms of physical experience.

With the bus fare came a possible bonus, which meant a lot in August 1990, during the post-war

period of rations and low supplies. If you bought a bus ticket on a summer's day in Tehran you'd already paid for a mobile sauna session. The bonus was the potential for the sauna to turn into a steam room. If a small number of passengers boarded the bus, dry heat might prevail. But with each additional passenger getting onto the moving spa, the humidity level grew. On a bus filled with passengers you were guaranteed the full steam room experience.
There was another attraction to boarding a full bus. Buses in Iran were traditionally a segregated means of travel. Men occupied the front and women the back. As with many such rules, this subdivision was not carried out on an egalitarian principle, nor did it take account of demographic realities. Almost two-thirds of the space was designated male territory. Bars were put in place to make sure division was practically enforced and morality preserved. It was only natural that women invaded the men's section at busy times. When the bus was really full, it felt as if the spa manager had turned up the heat to maximum and forgotten there were perishable humans inside, requiring both oxygen and residual hydration.

To get to the park where I played football with my friends, I always got on the bus at the beginning of its route. On this particular day all the windows of the bus were open, but in only a few minutes I felt sweat drops travelling all the way from my temples to my chin, armpits to navel. I was standing in the open space towards the back of the male area. As the bus filled up, I had to retreat, move all the way to the window and submit to being carried by the crowd this way and that. It happened only a few stops from the park. The bus was still quite full, but there was a bit of breathing space. I was looking out the window when I felt something soft and rounded touching my buttocks. It moved rhythmically, and with it I felt the front of my trousers beginning to stick out. I knew what was happening counted as sinful, but I liked it. I liked it so much I was scared to turn around and risk losing it. I'd heard stories. Navid brought "super" magazines to the park every week and we all hid under an old weeping willow and looked at those forbidden pictures in amazement and desire.

I adjusted the bag containing my football boots to my front, trying to conceal my response. I closed my eyes and thought of the naked girls I'd seen in those pages: German girls, Swedish girls, English girls, Japanese girls. But the girl who was rubbing her bottom against mine with so much intention was an Iranian schoolgirl. I could tell by the little bit of the dusty, cotton and polyester uniform I could see in my peripheral vision that she must be in high school, a couple of years older than me. I was aching to turn and look at her, but scared that people might notice what we were up to if I did. Summoning my most innocent expression, I glanced around as though to get my bearings and managed a forty-five degree turn to the right. Now I could see that she was taller than me and was indeed wearing the navy *manto* and head covering falling to the chest that girls her age were expected to wear to school. Body draped, her round face was left exposed to absorb all the sun. She didn't look like any of the girls in the magazines, but in my new position she managed to grab hold of my hand and press it. Was it a warning? Was she angry with me? As I considered these options, the crowd suddenly pushed us towards the wall.

Now we were standing side by side, but somehow my opened hand was caught between her soft bum and the hard bus wall. I didn't know what to do. My hand, the whole of my arm, my complete being felt paralysed. I was afraid that if I moved my hand she'd get upset and make a noise. I didn't want to be caught. It would be awful, the thirteen-year-old son of a war martyr touching a strange girl's buttock on the bus, in public, in broad daylight. Could there be anything worse?

She kept moving her body slowly. Her left arm was rubbing against my right shoulder; by the terms of our strange dance, it was her turn to make a new contact angle. A turn of only thirty degrees to the left meant that she was driving me crazy with her breast. Wasn't she wearing anything under her uniform?

Thanks to summer her nipple was caressing my arm where my short sleeve ended. There were only two things I wanted in the world at that very moment: I wanted the driver to brake hard, and for it to be suddenly night-time and all of Tehran swallowed in darkness. There have been very few occasions in my life when I have been grateful for the mysterious rhythms and spurts of Tehran traffic, but for once it worked for my pleasure. As the urge to give full attention to that bare nipple became alarmingly compelling, the bus suddenly jolted to a brutal stop, and yes, she was rubbing my entire front with her front for three seconds. Her conspiratorial smile told me that she knew how I felt.

I could stay no longer. With the sports bag clutched where it was required, I ran awkwardly down the steps of the bus and up the street. I'd already missed my stop and stayed on the bus for eight more, quite a long way. But on that day I ran all the way to the park where there was a pond filled with weed and gold fish and ducks, and I jumped right into it with the bag still glued to me. Two guards thought I was trying to mess with their authority and dragged me out and 'taught me a lesson' by repeatedly pinching my ears. I didn't mind; I had cleansed my body.

First published in the Erotic Review Magazine.

New Year's Eve

The three of them were talking about shoes, oblivious to the commotion around them. Or maybe they were playing a game involving feet raised and shaken. They were almost in silhouette from where I sat, with the fireplace in the background. I knew only one of them, Petra, and as she was a fashion stylist, I thought I was making a safe assumption about the shoes.

The party was in full swing, although midnight was three hours away. In one corner was a makeshift bar, with a massive block of ice that the white-frocked barman chipped bits off of for individual drinks. In the opposite corner a DJ was stationed with all her devices and kit. Across from the DJ was a cast-iron spiral staircase leading to the upper floor.

Petra's friend wasn't wearing a bra. Even the dimmed lighting couldn't deflect my recognition of the perky nipples that raised her satin dress. She was the tallest of the three and wore the shortest dress of her team. I was across from her, sitting on a felt sofa that I was stroking with one hand and whilst conveying an excellent whisky sour to my lips with the other. The barman, who was rumoured to be working at the Savoy Hotel, would certainly make his swanky employer proud. It was a perfectly balanced drink. As I was enjoying the view I realised that Perky Nipples was smiling at me. I must have been staring at her. I raised my glass and silently toasted her, holding her gaze.

It was at that moment that it happened to be her turn to raise her foot. Before doing so, she exchanged yet another glance with me, as if to command my closer attention, and I think she even bit her lip. Laughing, she raised her foot, and her thighs parted, so that it was quite clear that beneath the satin of her dress was only soft skin. Yes, it was dark down there and I couldn't see a great deal, but that much was quite clear. She was enveloped in satin for the party and nothing else. As she watched the thought pass over my face, we laughed simultaneously. That alerted Petra to what was going on and she waved me over to join them.

"Hey Petra!"

"How come you're keeping a low profile? Not at all like you."

"I was just enjoying the view," I said, and that

was absolutely true.

"Sneaky! Meet my friends. Eloise, this is Malcolm."

"Hello Eloise," I said.

"And Malcolm, this is Ursula."

"Oh yes, I may not know her name, but I have a feeling we're old friends already. I took her hand and she assumed I was going to kiss it, but instead, I raised her from the cube chair. "Let's get a drink." I led the way, still holding her hand. "What do you fancy?"

"Vodka and tonic, please."

"Are you sure you don't want to give this man's talents a try? He is pretty capable, I hear, of making you something a little more complicated than that."

"I have no doubts about his abilities. I just believe some things need to be kept simple."

"I see. Not wearing knickers is a part of the same philosophy?"

"Absolutely," Ursula said, and ran her index finger over the ice block, presumably to make sure that it was real. "That is if you know exactly what you want."

"And what is it that you want exactly, if I may enquire?"

"I'm so glad you asked." She turned to face me suddenly, her face alight. "When midnight strikes and the new year draws in, I want to sit on a man's face right in front of that fire and I want him to kiss my thighs and pussy until I moan in front of everybody. After that I want to sit on his lap and kiss him and taste myself in his mouth. I might even open his zipper and kiss him while he finds his way inside me."

"That is very precise. And what is the criteria for application?"

"Easy. I'll choose the soberest man. I like it stiff."

With no hesitation I poured my fresh whisky sour on the tip of the pristine ice block, earning myself an immediate remonstrance from the barman. He began pouring water over the ice to clean it. I turned back to her.

"I like men who show initiative. And that was your second already."

"How well you notice."

"How can you get what you want if you don't notice?"

"Very true. But let me tell you something. I can't help but notice that you are young."

"So? You are young, too."

"Yes, I know. But if I said YOLO, I would sound ridiculous. If you said it, it would be cute."

"Oh shut up, I'm not an underage teenager." She slapped me on the arm.

"I am most sincerely glad of that, but, let me put it this way, you sound too mature for your age. And then there is this innocence in your face. I can't put the two together."

She shook her head and taking my hand led the way up the spiral staircase. It was so narrow that I had to follow behind her. I slowed down in order to savour the skimming motion of her dress as it slid and hitched and redraped itself around her buttocks as she climbed the stairs. It was a mesmerising little play.

The stairs led to a small mezzanine with desks on two sides, occupied by party animals intent on rather predictably deviant activities. At the end of the room, through a small window, was a roof terrace. I gestured Ursula to go first as I didn't want to miss a single angle of the show.

"What are you, sixteen?" she jokingly told me off, but went ahead.

"Much younger, at heart." I shot back.

"I'm sure. Follow me then." She said wryly over her shoulder.

Most of the smoking guests occupied the tiny terrace, with nothing but thick ropes around it as protection. Ursula found a little spot, just about big enough for the two of us. Facing east, I put my arms around her, the palms of my hands on her stomach. She covered my hands with hers and slowly moved them up, until my hands fully cupped her breasts. They were a perfect round shape, but very soft, so soft that I was surprised that they could hold such a sprightly stance. The nipples, however, strained out from the softness of the creamier flesh, in opposition against my hands: firm, sturdy; strong.

She turned her head slightly towards me and looked into my eyes for a moment. The light from the streetlights below was flung strangely across her face, so that her eyes were shadowed and I couldn't read the expression in them. Then she turned around without a word and fought her way through the smokers, slipped back in through the window. I was not entirely sure what had happened, but I didn't think I'd done anything wrong. I wasn't even certain if she had had enough of me, or if it was calculated build up.

I stood there and stared at the skyscrapers in the distance and considered her voice. It carried authority and determination, a kind of self-assuredness that normally comes with age. Where did she find hers? I was sure she was at least ten years younger than me.

I made my way back down through the increasingly heaving and well-oiled crowd. The music had turned smooth and the lights even dimmer. From the middle of the staircase I saw Ursula and Eloise dancing cheek to cheek. By the time I was back on the floor, they were lost in each other's embrace, in one another's mouths.

It was only a few minutes to midnight. I was looking out of the window, pretending to be in my own world. But in reality I was staring at her reflection in the glass, fantasising about midnight and hoping I'd be the soberest man in the house. Most of the guests were on their way to the tiny roof terrace to get a glimpse of the fireworks, with the exception of a few who were either too drunk or not drunk enough to care. Would she follow through?

I saw Ursula's reflection get up and with that my heart started thumping like a green teenager's. She danced her way up to me and her arms slid round my waist and held me from behind. Now I could feel those hard nipples rubbing against my back.

"Looks like you're sober enough for my scenario," she said.

"I sure hope so."

"What are you waiting for then?"

She dragged me to the felt one-seater and sat me on it. She was tall enough to drape the short skirt of her dress over my head and force all that delicious, pink goodness onto my face. I loved her strength and ran my fingers under her thighs, not as forcefully as she, but enough to tell her how much I wanted to taste her. I could hear the sound of the fireworks going off outside and I was drunk on the slick of her, by which time her whole body was shaking like a butterfly drunk with candlelight.

For a man, there is not a single thing more beautiful in the world than the tremors of a woman against his touch. If transcendence exists, it is in that moment, when he takes his time and gives his woman an orgasm. There is nothing more vulnerable, more meditative, more life affirming.

But for Ursula once was not enough. She raised her legs a little, just enough for Eloise to sneak in. She kissed me once and without a moment of hesitation began to lick Ursula's pussy in a completely different way than I had. I must admit I had never seen that sight in real life and it was, without a doubt, one of the sexiest things I'd ever been party to: gentle but intent, without any awkwardness or strangeness. Ursula slid down slowly and sat astride my lap, unbuttoning my shirt as Eloise took my shoes off. I was undressed with efficient urgency – not that I had any objection – with a passion in both of them that drove me absolutely crazy. Ursula and Eloise seemed to take less care with each other's clothes, kissing and tearing with abandon, caressing each other's bodies so tenderly it looked like a choreographed art installation.

To watch that would have been enough, but clothes and kisses dispatched, they suddenly approached me from both sides, took my hands and raised me to standing, then knelt next to each other, my cock dancing between their mouths, with lips that were cool and tongues that rolled over my skin and nails that skittered like feathers over my most tender flesh. As it happened I felt confused, in an elated way, with the magnitude of the experience. Was I the luckiest man on earth?

Concerto

It is precisely at two o'clock every afternoon that Amandine sets out her chair and the waist-high wooden table under the weeping willow. The table stands to her right and holds a jug of water and a glass, a bowl of pistachios, and a green vase with a solitary flower that she picks just before the ceremony. She then brings the cello case and places it upright by the table, removes the instrument and sits facing the Pyrenees.

It is miles between her and the mountains. The lush grass covers the gap that is punctuated by odd houses and many cattle. The field in front of her holds the audience: the horses that she cares for, nurtures, feeds, caresses and plays for. The solo performance takes forty-five minutes.

The horses are not the only ones she cares for. Amandine looks after her father, 'a very tired man,' in her own words. This combined caring for horses and man she does partly as a hobby, partly out of grateful duty, or at least that is how it appears. Work, however, is entirely a different matter, although it too, is concerned with caring.

She normally takes only a single booking each weekend: one patient who gets all her attention, all her tutelage. Sometimes, very rarely, and almost only if they are return patients that she likes, she allows parties of up to three. Very rarely. It doesn't happen more than three or four times a year. She finds it exhausting to tend to more than one patient over a weekend. Besides, she has her personal life that requires copious amounts of time and energy.

When she has groups she has to ask Lucie to come and help with her father and the upkeep of the house. But Lucie comes with more disadvantages than the reverse. She is a sloppy cook who likes frying. That leaves the worktops in the kitchen covered in a film of oil droplets of astonishing diameter. When Lucie goes grocery shopping, she buys miniature plum tomatoes, donut peaches, and pro-bio or whatever-it-is-called yogurt. Amandine hates all that and the heaps of *chocolatine* brought back home. What is wrong with plain croissants and normal tomatoes and peaches and yogurt? Even if she can forgive all these lapses of taste, sixty-three year old Lucie's enthusiasm for talking is incomprehensible to Amandine. Why did her parents name her Lucie anyway? It was certainly not a name fashionable at that time.

It is most of all the talking that Amandine cannot tolerate. Even when she agreed to leave her musical life behind her to come and care for her father, she only bought her ticket after receiving assurances from the doctor at the nursing home that her father was in no way capable of speech. She could deal with virtually anything, cope with all the pain of seeing her father wither, slowly evaporate into the air, but only if the inexorable action of slow decrepitude were contained by the bubble of silence. The man had talked enough of his talks when healthy, it seemed to Amandine; had said things no human, least of all a daughter, should have been forced to hear. She would look after him only if he was never to utter a word again, not even one.

Amandine believes in taking things as they are, in accepting. But when it comes to words, she tolerates no sacrilege. Words are tender vehicles, capable of delivering healing of a potency that no other medicine can replicate. Equally they can carry crimes of a violence that could be committed by no other means. Insufficient awareness around words and you are guaranteed to work your own undoing. Her father had committed this deadly sin and, as a result, never heard a word from his daughter again. Even now that Amandine is his carer, she speaks not a word. She comes into his room in silence, changes his sheets and diapers and clothes; rubs his muscles gently, but utters not a sound. She opens the curtains and lets the sunshine in, opens the windows and hears the symphony of the world outside. Her father hears that too, but nothing from Amandine.

Although it is the second week of April, in the morning the hedges are covered in frost, which is not customary for the time of the year. In the fields, clouds come out of horses' mouths. Even they seem undecided if the winter has finally gone. Amandine is expecting a patient for the weekend. As a matter of principle, she uses fresh horsehair for each patient. She likes mixing hair from at least four different animals, for each horse has a different temperament, spicing up the end result. She goes hair foraging among the horses only after playing for them, as she finds them more relaxed. She pats them on the back, talks to them, strokes their beautiful faces and then takes hair from their tails.

From the time Amandine greets the patients till the moment they leave, they only see her in elegant equestrian gear: a crisp, high-collared white shirt with two buttons on the neck, a black, show jacket with narrow, ivory trims on the collar, knee-high leather boots, also in black, over a pair of tight, white breeches. Her riding hat is in navy velvet and is complete with a padded, leather chinstrap.

There are four buildings on the property. Upon arrival, Amandine shows her patients to *Chez Sandrine*, the house halfway between the stables and the residence where Amandine and her father live. *Chez Sandrine* used to be a bed and breakfast years ago, but is now only used by the weekend patients. It has a grand fireplace in the living room and a set of light mustard, velvet sofas. The master bedroom has its own bathtub, from which you can stare straight out at the mountains, not that Amandine ever uses it.

Behind the stable lies the fourth building, a decrepit-looking barn. But inside it is a different story. Amandine has personally refurbished the interiors. On the long wall she has assembled four bays punctuated by mounts for canes, crops, paddles and whips. She has an impressive number of each, but Amandine prefers the ones she has made by hand: the paddles out of wood and leather and the horsehair whips. She feels that she is cheating her patients if she uses tools that she hasn't personally invested her time and emotion in making.

The process of creating the tools puts her in a very good mood; it is a reminder of the months spent observing in the workshop of the master Parisian luthier, learning the ins and outs of her instrument, how every tiny element was assembled to elicit the perfect timbre. Sometimes late at night she would wander through the workshop, when the luthier was absorbed in some tricky task, stroking the grain of the wood in the half finished instruments, or examining bows yet to be stringed, trying to imagine how they would sound.

The opposite wall is home to ropes at one end, in a variety of thicknesses and colours. The short wall opposite the entrance exhibits cuffs and collars and leads; harnesses and gags.

In the central space within stands a medical examination chair, an upright reticulated wall made of thick metal bars, and a wooden platform perfect for lying patients face down, bottom up, arms raised to the back and their neck, arms, feet and thighs tightly tied, secured to metal pipes, each carefully arranged to make the possibility of movement a wild dream.

Amandine is exigent with her patients. They come to her for pain and that is exactly what she dishes out in abundance. She is generous to them with the extremity of her strikes and with the tightness of her knots. A perfectionist from the cradle, Amandine never changes. It doesn't matter what she does, she wants to excel; she wants to give it all she's got, the best of her talents and abilities.

Amandine's relationship with the cello is her private affair. In her life before, it didn't matter where she played, what piece or before which audience. It was the nature of running her fingers over the spruce top, flirting with the strings that were once inside a sheep, and performing the slow brutalisation of the horsehair on the bow. How many bows had she ruined in her time? She was notorious for going through two or three in some concerts.

When she held the cello close, it didn't matter if she was playing in Carnegie Hall, the Hall of Mirrors at Versailles, or the Berliner Philharmonie (at all of which she had been warmly received on repeated occasions). She didn't even seem to register that the trajectory of her musical career only ascended. What mattered was the intense conversation that took place between the cello and Amandine.

When the time came for her to depart Berlin so that she could become the carer for her father, the abrupt departure of a genius cellist was headline news. But Amandine barely registered the storm. She did what needed to be done, with dispatch.

This patient owns a hedge fund in Geneva that services twenty clients, ranging from royals to oligarchs to philanthropists. He is a regular. Amandine likes the change that she sees happen to Mark every time he visits, although she is aware that he has a long way to go. When he arrives, he is confident, in his sharp suit and colourful tie, the epitome of authority. After only a few minutes in the barn he starts mellowing down. It doesn't take much flogging to get him screaming. Sometimes Amandine has to go out of her way and instruct Mark firmly to shut up. He cries the width of his face and begs to be given mercy, but that product does not exist on these premises. He of all people knows that, after seventeen visits in less than two years. He most of all, knows that his screams and tears only fuel Amandine to administer her treatment faster and harder, to aim at the tender flesh, where it hurts the most.

The first three times that Mark came to *Chez Sandrine,* he told his family that he was travelling on business. The downside to this story, however, was his instruction to Amandine: no marks. She found such limitation desperately dull and declined, after the third visit, to take Mark's booking.

"I refuse to be treated with disrespect. This house has its rules. If you cannot comply, you shall not be admitted," she had told Mark on the phone, in a voice that she kept composed, with some effort.

Mark had shortly thereafter realised that he didn't want to do this half-heartedly. He had managed to pluck up the courage and confess his needs to his wife. To his surprise, she hadn't even raised an eyebrow. 'Do what you have to do,' she had responded.

"I will come back, each time, with marks. Before the welts get enough time to heal, I will go back to *Chez Sandrine*. I want to make sure that the sight will in no way be unsavoury to you." He had said, rather formally.

How much had she wanted to say that she wished to be the one administering the flogging! Alas, Mark's wife had been brought up with so much guilt that even the spark of a thought like that in her head required strenuous repentance. Although Mark shared the same style of upbringing as his wife and might have suffered pangs of guilt himself had he engaged in more traditional amours, his discovery of Amandine freed him from such psychic woes. Mark's proclivities might have forced him to confess to a priest; but, he reasoned, since the punishment meted out for his 'sin' might have been the same as the sin itself in more extreme religious circles, he felt that his sin and atonement were in some sense simultaneous. It was a highly efficient paradigm that pleased him endlessly. His wife, whose formation was less Aquinian than her husband's, wondered at his endless ability to square his conscience. Mark considered his wife's thoughts not at all.

The barn had fallen into desuetude before Amandine carried out her transformation. Hook by hook, block by block, she had turned The Grange into the care home for her patients. After three months of hard graft, when every element was firmly in place and all the ropes and crops were hung from their designated places, she had walked through it and run her fingers over them, looked at every tool and line carefully and made sure no trace of imperfection could be found in the sanctuary that she had created.

She knew one thing immediately; that she had never felt so accomplished in doing anything. The sense of achievement so overwhelmed her that, for a second, Amandine felt her legs had mysteriously hollowed out, suddenly incapable of carrying her light weight. But such fragility was short lived.

Mark is quiet, so is Amandine, the only sound her footfalls as she strides up and down the barn. He is tied to the reticulated wall, facing the ropes. The air inside The Grange is cool and has a powdery quality to it, as if a vaporiser has squirted out the essence of grass and pine. None of the sharp, afternoon sunshine is allowed in, but Amandine glows in the darkened room. Mark imagines how she might look without the uniform, uncovered to him. He is profoundly glad that for all her talents, Amandine has not yet mastered telepathy.

Amandine swirls the handmade whip in the air. The horsehair makes a slight hiss, enough to make all the hair on the back of Mark's neck stand up. She does it again and Mark's heart pounds so furtively he is scared it might jump out and leave the husk of his body, heartless in the chamber.

The first strike is always gentle, exploratory, as one tests the temperature of ocean shallows before jumping in for a full dip. But that first one is the most delicious of all the strikes for Mark, so tantalising that it sends shockwaves through the entirety of his nervous system. He has decided to be strong on this visit, to be good and make no sound, to show Amandine that although submitting to her is his one and only desire, he can grow stronger and stronger, withstand more of her power. If only he can manage that for once: a whole session without sounding like a helpless victim. Ten minutes in and sweat drops cover his face, travel down his body. So far, the only sound he has made is his hard breathing. No screams yet.

Amandine, after seventeen sessions, is not used to this. She has yet to find anyone with as low a tolerance to pain as Mark. Maybe change is possible after all with persistence.

Amandine's father was not a bad man. He was stubborn, just north of normal and set in his ways. When he made a decision to do something in a certain way, he found it extremely difficult to change his mind, to alter the plan. He bred horses for a living. But young Amandine didn't care about those traits. He has been her father and mother, the mother that she never met, because she had died while giving birth to Amandine.

For many years Amandine would sit in her room, staring at the picture of the woman whose hair was more golden than the sunshine, whose eyes were kinder than all of their horses combined. She would stare at the photograph and apologise to her mother for causing her untimely death. The apologies never came out of her mouth, they were all in her heart, pumped through her veins and pricked like tiny needles into each of her cells.

When news came that Amandine had been accepted to the Conservatoire de Paris her father was in the midst of currying one of the mares. Amandine could see that as she uttered the words, the circular motion of her father's grooming comb became harsh and erratic. The poor horse began making noises as the discomfort grew on her skin and blood began dripping down. Amandine could still hear the soft sound of the horse's pain and the faint sound of welling blood beneath her father's clenched hand. In her memory at least, the blood had a sound.

As on every Friday night, the inhabitants of her village, her friends and neighbours, gathered together for a drink and some fun and games. Amandine's father had sat in the corner of the cafe all evening and pronounced at least two bottles of Burgundy dead on his own. He had rejected any approach.

"Yes, I'm very excited about it," Amandine was telling one of her classmates when her father seemed suddenly to rouse himself.

"You are, aren't you? I would be excited too, to leave an old fool and get away from a place that stinks of horse-shit. What comparison is there anyway between this and Paris?" His voice was now the only one in the common room, raised to a level that had turned all present into an alert audience, hanging on each word.

"Why was I so witless to believe all these years that you would not turn whore for the city like your mother and leave me all on my own?"

Amandine had turned scarlet. Her father's words washed over her like a wave, rendering her utterly dumb. She had never been so confused in her life. Wasn't her mother dead? Didn't she die giving birth? In the silence she noticed that the villagers of her father's generation seemed to be staring fixedly at their feet. She had beaten herself up all these years thinking she was the cause of her own mother's death. Was that not true? What was he talking about?

"Why don't you go find her?" Her father slurred. "You should start to live together, be all nice and cosy. Do you want her address and telephone number? I'll dig it out for you."

Amandine couldn't listen anymore in that circle of faces. She ran out of the hot cafe and into the darkness. She ran the entire three miles home and didn't stop until she'd reached the stables and found her corner, warm with the smell of horse and dung and darkness.

Mark manages the entire fourteen-minute century without a shriek, a personal best. It is the knotted flogger descending on the back of his thighs, on the now tenderised flesh, stained with his sweat and blood, that puts a stop to his lucky streak. Amandine strikes and Mark cries, tears flow from an infinite source. They come so naturally to him that he forgets the pain. His sense of serenity and peace grows with every drop leaving his eyes. He loses track of time and pain. He is there to be there, to ensconce himself, to lose himself to the possibility of an existence outside the boundaries of the barn, his being contained within those walls, the great impossible world shrinking strike by strike to the drum of his heart, the blood humming along each stripe.

Amandine is the drug that he has searched for all of his life, he suddenly realises. Prozac, cocaine, Wellbutrin, ecstasy, Amitriptyline; none poses the slightest competition compared to the serotonin generated by Amandine's method. She should be given a Legion d'Honor for her services to humanity.

It is the Monday after Mark has left. Amandine sets the table under the willow tree. A white rose is to sit with her this afternoon. It is precisely at two o'clock that she pops open a bottle of champagne, pours herself a glass, takes a sip and stares out at the Pyrenees, which appear to be melting in the sunshine like honey.

"There will be no concert today," she calls out loud. She is sure the horses are very disappointed, but polite enough not to show it. She is sure that they understand her joy at releasing a patient permanently.

A Seagull in Louisiana

It was July. They sat on the dais of one of the sculptures and watched the sea. The sky was a crisp blue with a light scattering of clouds, the air so thin that Silja was sure she could see Sweden gleam under the sun some fourteen kilometres away on the other side of the waterway. Akari thought this was ludicrous. “It’s your imagination, silly,” she said. “How can anybody see that far?”

Silja had promised Akari this visit to the Louisiana Museum of Modern Art, (the one on the outskirts of Copenhagen) for a few years and when they found out about a special Yoko Ono exhibition, they both agreed that the time was right for a day out. But when they got there they were hungry, they wanted coffee, and then they were distracted by the sunshine that is rarely ever found that high up in the north. They settled beside the sculpture and caught up on the stories that they owed each other. Since graduating they had busied themselves with work and all the rest of that grown up stuff and didn't get the chance to meet up as often as they used to.

Right in the middle of Akari's account of how her sister had finally decided to move to the countryside and forget about the hustle and bustle of the big city, Silja noticed a guy checking them out and being very obvious about it. She pretended that she didn't see him and for once her sunglasses came in useful. It didn't take him long to come and sit on the same step, leaving enough space in the middle that it wouldn't look suspect, but close enough that he could engage Silja and Akari. They kept on talking and he was quiet. Maybe Silja had misread him. Maybe he was just after the sea views. Amid Silja's analysis a seagull came and sat between her and the stranger, who grabbed his opportunity without hesitation.

"Oh boy, I never thought of Danish birds as being so intrusive."

Their feathered friend departed but the conversation continued, briskly moving away from birds. He said a lot very quickly and asked as many questions. Silja soon learnt that he was from New York, taught economics, and was on a one-year sabbatical in Paris. Now that he had the chance, he wanted to visit as much of Europe as he could and that was just what he did most weekends – visited friends in various cities and proved to them that there were some Americans who did actually own a passport.

"But why do you sound so British?" Silja asked.

"Oh that. Causes less aggravation when travelling. The old Empire isn't disdained as much as the new eh?"

In the middle of the friends' laughter and the American's non-stop talking, a couple sat down just where the seagull had entertained them with its presence. The American looked at the newcomers as if they were war criminals. Standing up, he walked away without saying a word, grabbed two chairs from one of the nearby tables and placed them very close to the girls' legs; he sat right in front of Silja.

"It would be rude if I kept talking over the... impediment. By the way, I'm Eric." And he shook Silja's hand.

"Hello Eric. Silja... and this is my friend Akari."

"Why did you bring two chairs?" said Akari as they shook hands.

"Oh, this is for my friend who I have tasked with sourcing caffeine. I'm staying with him in Frederiksberg."

"You live on the wrong side, buddy," said Akari with an exaggerated American accent. Her joke was intended more for Silja than for Eric: the old rivalry of neighbourhoods.

"I thought that was the best part of

Copenhagen," he said.

"It is technically not Copenhagen," Silja said. "It is a different municipality. But it is much more pleasant than the rest of Copenhagen, new neighbour!"

"Brilliant, you live there too. Maybe you and I can do a deal. You show me the best bar in the area and I'll buy you a drink."

It was quick and it was forward. And it was certainly not what a Danish guy would do, ever. Silja liked it.

"Deal," she said. She could see Akari's side look. She couldn't see her eyes, but she knew that Akari had put on that cute round-eyes-in-motion face, pretending to be shocked, but at the same time admiring her.

Eric's friend joined them with two cups of coffee. An offer of a lift back to the city was made and declined, since Eric and his friend had finished looking round Louisiana while Akari and Silja's visit hadn't even begun. But a plan was put in place for meeting later in the evening. Eric had already extracted Silja's number and given her a business card.

Her apartment was small, but every item was selected tastefully. A round dining table stood by a sofa upholstered in fine grey wool. Floor lamps were the only form of lighting, which made the room atmospheric but didn't aid investigation of the wall full of books.

"Do you really live here?" Eric asked. "This is too pretty, too clean: like a high-end showroom."

"I hope not, everything here has a soul! But you're in Scandinavia, remember?"

She told him stories about each piece. One, about a side table that she had inherited from a great grandmother, Eric found particularly interesting. It had been made in 1910 in the suburbs of Copenhagen and still had the robust gleam of strong design that had experienced appropriate use. Silja grabbed a bottle of Chardonnay from the fridge and sat by Eric on the sofa. He stroked her hair and let the scent of her.... was it her perfume, shampoo, her skin... tickle his nostrils. He couldn't tell what it was, but her scent reminded him of a drizzly day in New York; a long walk, the reflection of lights on a wet pavement; a small girl being dragged along by her mother, focused on getting the right amount of candy floss in her mouth. He remembered the sound of jazz combined with the noise of the traffic. He zoned back in. Silja was talking about her great grandmother.

"Her name was Sofia. Her lover was killed in the war, the First World War. She found out that she was pregnant three days after an old officer had knocked on the door. He wore a huge handlebar moustache and delivered the bad news from the Front along with a shoe box of my great grandfather's belongings: a name tag, a picture of my great grandmother, a wallet, a can opener, and a few other bits and bobs. She cried her eyes out for a month and then decided to get on with it. She never married and the son that was born, my grandfather, grew up in the suburbs without ever knowing his father."

"How do you know all this?" Eric asked her.

"I found her diary in the bottom drawer," she pointed at the chest and refilled his glass.

"Let's pretend we are them."

"What?"

"Let's pretend this is the last time they are together before the lover goes to war. Let's pretend we have all the emotions that they felt that day: the uncertainty, the fear, the love. Let's make love like this is our last chance."

"You are mad," Silja said, and then went silent. She touched his fingertips with hers and raised her hand, his hand floating with it as if they were magnetically attached. "But I will share in your madness tonight."

She put her wine glass down and leaned forward. Her kiss, the warmth of her breath, and her scent again. Eric had never found anybody's lips as delicate. He tried to imagine, to put himself in that lover's place over a century ago. His imagination took over and he could even hear the shelling, the hum of bullets overhead. He had to tell his imagination he was not in the frontline just yet, that this was supposed to be the day before mobilisation. But it didn't listen.

They didn't bother shutting the blinds or turning the lights off. Silja ripped Eric's clothes off with a passionate intensity that he had only rarely encountered before. He reciprocated, then lay on his back on the felt sofa and watched her beautiful body move over him like a wave, with Copenhagen still and silent beyond the window. The sound of the ocean overcame the wartime noises of death and departure. And he vanquished the dreadful feeling that this could be their last night together: that there might be no coming back.

Eric stood naked by the window and watched the distant lights of the harbour. Life was running through his veins at high speed. Copenhagen was asleep. Silja lay, eyes closed, flushed and folded on the sofa. Somewhere, Eric felt, in the very same moment, a lover was gazing at a photograph of his sweetheart before going over the top. And it seemed to him that time had stretched somehow. He looked back from the window at Silja's sleeping face. Perhaps it was only the harbour light, but as he glanced to the table above her head, he saw that her smile was the same as the one that stood, locked in time, smiling from the photograph.

First published in the Erotic Review Magazine.

For a calm, September day, the flight has been unusually turbulent. From his 28F seat, not quite the tail, but not too far off, he watches the khaki runway and takes a deep breath. His fidgety fellow passenger tries to peek through, squashing his shoulder in the process. The landing gives him a last full-body shaking.

"Welcome to Imam Khomeini International Airport. The outside temperature is 29 degrees celsius and there is a northeasterly breeze. May I remind you that alcoholic beverages are strictly prohibited in Iran. Enjoy your stay in Tehran or if you are transiting, have a safe onward journey."

The endless corridor is narrow, half the floor in cheap granite, the other half consumed with the travelator. The ceiling is low, a lot lower than Schiphol and Heathrow and Kastrup. His left hand drags the soft, grey suitcase on its two wheels; his right hand clutches his passport. He thinks he shouldn't have drunk the small glass of merlot at the start of the flight. He hopes the guard won't smell it on his breath.

Twenty minutes in the queue and he finds himself in front of the young officer with two stars on each shoulder of a nicely fitted uniform. "Salam" he says and gets the same in response. His passport is scanned and his details are checked. He feels his heart racing. The officer is looking intently on the screen and goes through the pages of the passport, every visa, every stamp, but not even a brief look at the owner. It is the sound of the entry stamp that gives him the permission to breathe again. He takes the passport back, unceremoniously, casually, without much fuss. "Merci," he says, in the fashion of most urban Iranians, with a soft, rolling 'r' and walks slowly around the cubicle.

He is halfway down the crawling steps of the escalator that he hears his name on the loudspeaker. Is he imagining it or is it really happening? No, there is his name again; and the instruction to report to the information desk. As he steps off the escalator and onto the floor, he feels as if his heart has fallen into his stomach, nauseated and a little dizzy. He does as ordered, goes to the counter and says his name. The soft-spoken woman asks him to wait, dials a number and announces his name. A man runs down the escalator and gets to the information desk as quickly as he can. He is bespectacled, scruffy and out of breath. He doesn't waste any time, "your passport," he demands. "Follow me," is his next statement. The agent leads him upstairs back to the same level where passport control supposedly cleared the visitor to enter.

The agent goes into a small room and invites him to take a seat while he continues going through the pages of the passport and making notes. When he asks what is going on, the agent makes a placatory gesture, but remains silent. At last, the agent stretches his arms, makes another note and hands him a piece of paper, a receipt with his passport details.

"You should go to an interview on Saturday," he says, which is in a week's time and not part of the weekend in Iran.

"What interview? What is the problem?"

"Why do you think there is a problem?" the agent asks, with a smirk on his face.

Now on his feet, he slaps the back pocket of his jeans twice: "Because my passport is not here. And my return flight is at 3 a.m. on Sunday."

"Don't worry, it's just a few questions. You should be fine to get to your flight. But you can call the number on the receipt if you want an earlier appointment."

His yellow cab races down the highway towards his family's neighborhood. The sky is not as clear as he hoped it would be, neither is his head. The golden dome of the ayatollah's mausoleum shines from the distance. Cars overtake one another as if something better than a traffic jam awaits them. He asks the driver to put Radio Payam on, so he can try and calm down to some chill out music, tunes modified, vocals chopped off, so that they adhere to the Islamic code. The music doesn't work. What if they don't give his passport back, don't let him leave? How about his life back in Brussels, his beautiful beagle Charlie only booked into the kennel for a week?

After embracing every family member on arrival, he puts his index finger on his mouth and nose and makes them understand that they should hand in their mobile phones to him without saying a word. He dumps all the devices on one of the beds and covers them with a few pillows, comes out and closes the door, then herds the family to the farthest corner of the house from that bedroom and tells them what happened at the airport. For the sake of his family, he reassures them that it must be a mistake but best be safe.

"You never know if they use these phones to listen to our conversations."

After everybody goes to sleep, he has a quick look at his email. Then he opens Grindr, out of curiosity, just to see if it does work in Iran, if anybody is on it. He takes an unusual pleasure in realising that there are a lot of guys on the app, and some seriously hot ones. They must be courageous to be cruising on a gay app in a country that could hang you for homosexuality. He first inserts the disclaimer on his profile: "In 021 until Saturday. Get in line, boys!" He likes several of the candidates and it doesn't take long to get the first match.

"And where can one find you after Saturday, mister?" opens the conversation.

"Oh, that's a secret I cannot disclose," he replies.

"Why not? You'll have to kill me if you tell me?"

"Something like that ;)"

"So, we're gonna stick to the present?"

"That'd be ideal."

"Deal."

"Whereabouts do you live?"

"Bang in the centre, near Revolution Square."

"That sure brings back memories!"

"Did you go to Tehran University?"

"I did, and that makes me feel old. It was ages ago."

"Why don't you come refresh those memories?"

"I'm taking that as an invitation."

"You bet your sweet ass ;)"

"How about Saturday at 12:30?"

"Is that a hint that I am cooking lunch for you?"

"As long as it is not bloody *Ghormeh Sabzi*, yes!"

"Ha ha ha! Any other dietary requirements?"

"Not that I am aware of..."

His appointment is in an ordinary government building, the office for immigration and passports, at 10 a.m. Of course, the twist is that he is to go to the out building on one side, with a sign on the door saying "The President's Representative Office," code for the Intelligence. He is asked to take a seat in the waiting room that resembles one in a hospital, rows of green plastic chairs, nobody waiting apart from him. He is finally summoned to go into a room, where two men await him, one in a light grey suit, the other in a white shirt over his black trousers and sporting a thick beard. They both shake his hand and say hello.

"Who are your friends?" asks the suited man, without preamble. The other agent, younger, seems to be the junior. He has an A4 notepad in front of him and makes notes with a blue Bic.

He tries to speak, but his tongue has turned into dry wood with rough edges, it rubs against the rest of his mouth and he feels it will bleed any minute. He finally manages a few hardly audible words: "Can I get a glass of water, please?"

"Of course. I'll get them to bring you a nice cup of tea."

"Water, please."

Water comes and is consumed. The question is repeated.

"What do you mean?"

"I mean a list of all of your friends."

"I have lots of friends."

"And we have a lot of time. Actually, all the time in the world."

That statement scares him. What does it mean? Will they keep him? His flight is in 16 hours. Will he make it?

"But why am I here? What is the problem?"

"Why do you think there is a problem?"

It is still the man in the suit talking. The boy hasn't uttered a word.

"If there is not a problem, why am I here?"

"What's wrong with having a nice chat? You don't like chatting to us?"

How can he possibly answer that? He produces some random names that the young agent diligently notes down. Does he even know how to spell non-Persian names? There is no question about what he does, what his life is, or why he is back. It's all about his friends.

"Look, I honestly don't know what you are after. But one thing I'm sure about is that I have no skills or interests in keeping with your line of work."

"Is that so?" asks the suited agent in a tone that has changed from softly interested to one invested with several shades of dread. He stops talking and watches his prey, lets him suffer under the gaze, sweat drop by drop. His blood roars in his ears. "Get out of my sight!" The agent suddenly shouts, and it is over.

Startled, he gets to his feet shakily and looks first at one and then the other of the two agents. Swallows. Decides to try, "But how about my passport?"

"Out!"

He goes out to the waiting room with all that a confiscated passport means marching through his head in fast-forward. The young agent follows him out soon enough, fortunately, and puts an end to that trail of miserable thought.

"It's OK, don't worry. My colleague can have a temper at times. You're cleared and will get your passport back."

So, you're the good cop on time delay, he thinks.

"My flight is in 15 hours or so. Isn't my passport here?"

"No, but it's absolutely fine. Somebody will deliver it at three o'clock."

"What do you mean by deliver it?"

“Be at this address,” the agent says, handing him a scrap piece of paper. “There is a park bench at the corner of the main road and the small alleyway. Be on time.” He shakes his hand once again and goes back into the interrogation room.

He stands there, puzzled. He looks at the address and remembers that it is a couple of minutes’ walk from the headquarters of the Ministry of Intelligence, a brutalist building with very tall walls, Soviet style, give or take.

He hops into a shared cab in the direction of the Revolution Square, where he is meeting his date, Ramin. He sits in the front and checks his phone. He feels the throbbing in both of his temples. Was it a good idea to arrange a hook up for today?

Ramin is well built, with a jaw that resembles Rodin sculptures. He greets him at the door to his flat. He smells like the duty free perfume shop, in a very pleasant way. He speaks Persian with a sweet Isfahan accent that gives each word a twirl or a stretch. They enter into an open plan living room with a kitchen located at the far end.

“Can I have your phone, please?”

A little taken aback, Ramin asks why.

He puts his index finger over his mouth, hinting silence is required and extends his hand to take Ramin's phone. He obliges, but seems to be alarmed. He takes his own mobile phone out of his pocket and puts both phones in the fridge.

"What the hell are you doing that for?"

"I'm sorry, this looks mental, but I am not crazy. I assure you." And he explains why he is doing that. That he is on his way back from interrogation, that his passport is somewhere held by Intelligence.

"Oh my God! But why? What have you done to deserve it?" Ramin's jaw has literally dropped and his eyes are alert. He finds it sweet to see all that fear in Ramin's face, a person that he has met just a minute ago caring enough about him to be so horrified on his behalf.

"Nothing. I live abroad. I have my own business. I have nothing to do with politics. I really don't know."

"Maybe it's just a mistake. Maybe your name is similar to somebody else's."

"Maybe. Or maybe they wanted to recruit me as a snitch."

"Oh my Lord! You didn't say yes, I hope. Mind you, it would be hot to fuck a spy."

"Hell no! I said I was otherwise preoccupied. I was thinking of you."

As intense as the situation is, that comment feels like a mountain breeze on a hot summer's day in Tehran, the breeze that reminds you there is life beyond the hell of forty-two degrees, that you shouldn't give up and drop dead right there and then. They laugh and agree to stop talking about all that shit.

Ramin strokes his hair and ear. They kiss on the sofa and undress one another.

"You smell divine," he tells Ramin and keeps sniffing his neck. There is a leathery quality to his skin, buttery soft. It reminds him of the boy he lost his virginity to in middle school. Young lovers, doing the loving hush hush, at every opportunity they found or created, during all the skipped lessons and imaginary basketball games.

They fuck against a north-facing window and to the phallic view of Milad Tower. He is surprised that he can get an erection with all that is on his mind.

They put on kitchen aprons instead of their clothes and eat sitting on their bare bums.

He notices that the time is coming to two o'clock.

"Shit, will I make it to the other side of the city in an hour?"

"The traffic shouldn't be too bad at this hour, but you better hurry."

He gets dressed as quickly as he can.

"Don't forget your phone," Ramin says. "Do you want me to go with you to the taxi stand?"

"No, you better not be seen with me. I may

sound a bit paranoid, but better be safe."

"It was great to meet you, crazy man!" Ramin says by the door as they kiss goodbye.

"You too, scented bender."

As he steps out of the building, a motorbike hoots at him. He's heard that some bikers work as taxis. Must be his lucky day. He jumps on the back of the Honda CGI 125, no helmet provided, but speed guaranteed.

He gets to the location twenty minutes too early. He sits at the bench and closes his eyes. What is going to happen? A van, five men in balaclavas and him pushed into the back and disappear for an uncertain amount of time? What else could be waiting for him?

The little park is adjacent to a highway heaving with cars and the roar of their engines, the refuse of their odorous gases, the madness of their drivers.

He hasn't told anyone that he is out there to get his passport. Nobody but Ramin.

At 3 p.m. sharp, he sees a man halting his motorcycle by the side of the smaller road, removing his helmet and walking towards him. He seems to have a limp right arm. Isn't he the guy who was at the reception of the interrogation place in the morning?

He comes and greets him warmly, shakes his hand with his left hand, and produces the passport. He feels his mouth has dried up again.

"Thank you," he says as he puts the passport

in his pocket.

"Don't worry, it's fine. What was it all about? Why did they want to talk to you?"

"I have absolutely no clue. They kept asking about my friends."

"Oh, that! Well, have a safe trip back to Belgium, son. And give me a receipt before you disappear."

"A receipt?"

"Yes, a receipt that I have returned your passport."

"Oh! But I don't have any paper. Or pen."

"Here," the man hands him a scrap of paper that he finds in one of his pockets. And a pen.

"What shall I write?"

"All your details and that you have received your document safe and sound."

He writes that down in a couple of lines, using the passport under the paper so that he can do the writing.

"Don't forget your passport number and your father's name."

Back at the airport, his heart is thumping. He is queuing for the passport control and he is in no way convinced that he will get the exit stamp. There are still a few people in front of him when he feels a hand tapping his shoulder. Startled, he flinches and turns around.

"Hey, are you OK?" says a man probably his age, a couple of inches taller, wearing an open neck, short sleeved shirt that displays his sculpted arms. "You seem stressed."

"No, no, no." He realises that he should control his nerves and slow down his words. "I have a lot on my mind, a lot to do when I get back."

"Where are you off to?"

"Brussels. I live there. How about you?"

"Ah, we're almost neighbours. I live in Paris."

"Shall we have a cup of coffee after passport control?"

"Caffeine doesn't agree with me much. Why don't you invite me for Belgian beer over a weekend?"

"Boy, you're quick. And I thought I held the record."

"Here's my card. Call me."

He looks at him, smiles, puts the card in his wallet and walks to the immigration officer.

Sushi for one

Between us is glass and 'fruit of the sea' on a bed of crushed ice. He carves out a thin slice of yellowtail and lightly places it on rolled rice. His final touch is *benidate*, the purple water pepper to add colour contrast and balance out the acidity of the fish. When he plays swords with his shiny knives, I am in two minds. Is he a monk and this ceremony his meditation, the way he chops and slices and forms and garnishes? Or is he just a child content with his toys, playing in the world of his imagination? I don't know. All I know is that I like both. Maybe he is somewhere between the two.

I am wearing my navy velvet dress that falls to just below the knee. He can't see my legs crossed and tucked at the ankle or my feet arched extravagantly in perfectly balanced stilettos. Across the neck of the dress the velvet recedes into lace, fitted to follow the plunge from collarbone to cleavage as close as skin. He might see some of this. If he looks my way, that is. I am sitting right across from him, maybe a metre-and-a-half apart, but he seems to be oblivious to the world outside his fish and rice. Or, perhaps, he is ignoring me.

He has his back to me, inspecting a dish that one of his staff is proffering. I can't see the dish, but I can tell that he is not entirely disappointed. He is calm, although the kitchen is heaving with activity this late in the evening. His short hair, combed to one side, shines with freshness with no sign of the fact that he must have started his shift ten hours ago.

A couple is sitting to my right. It must be their first date. The guy is wearing a white, open-neck shirt and blue jeans. How original! But it seems to work. I can smell his cologne from here. The girl, sitting between the guy and me is in a short, red dress, her nail varnish a perfectly calibrated scarlet match. I try to hear their conversation whilst keeping my head straight and my eyes glued to the chef. They are not from London, it's clear. They are staying in a nearby Mayfair hotel. Well done me for getting the first date thing absolutely spot on!

"How about we walk back and use the sauna before they close it?" The guy asks, and I wonder if he is German. Not that this is my best guessing night.

I can't hear what the girl says and I realise that

they cannot be from the same place and communicate in English. This small discovery feels much more of an accomplishment than it should in reality.

"Nay problem, let's have another drink then," he responds.

Is 'nay' a German-sounding 'no'? This guy confuses me.

Fortunately I am distracted by a little drama unfolding before my eyes. One of the junior chefs manages to slip. That alone can be a significant happening in a crowded kitchen, but the young man is carrying a tray with half a salmon on it. The fish flies through the air and lands on the chef's shoulder, tail up, pink side out, and slaps his chest with a splashing sound effect. The kitchen goes silent and time slides into slow motion. It feels as if the fish stays, levitating against the chef's pristine jacket for hours, but almost immediately it begins sliding, making an oozy path down the chef's body towards the floor. All watch with interest (including the chef himself). His eyes follow the trail, which now looks like a continuous watery line, painted down his side. Neither he nor the guilty minion attempt to catch the fish halfway. It slides all the way down to his waist, and as it hits the bump that is his belt, jerks again and somersaults flat onto the floor. There is an anxious silence as the kitchen braces for the brutal fate of their coworker. The chef coolly raises his head, measured as a lion from a fresh kill. As his eyes become level with the young man's, he bursts into laughter, with a noise that resembles the puncturing of a tire. The kitchen follows in uproarious relief. He taps the minion on the shoulder, who is smiling but looks very apologetic, head bowed down, and tells him it's no big deal.

"Make sure to chop off its wings next time so it doesn't fly again," he says, causing more laughter. He turns to his second in command, "Stop ordering flying fish; how many times have I told you?"

As the situation slips back to normal and the chef changes to a new set of whites, I hear my neighbours wrapping up the evening. I turn to them and say I couldn't help overhearing that they are staying at The Blue Fin.

"I have heard a lot about the place. How do you like it?"

"It's wonderful. We've had such a good time. Oh, and the beds are divine." The girl answers me with a wide smile.

"And the jacuzzi pumps all the stress out of your tissues. It's the strongest I've ever experienced," the guy jumps in.

"Do you happen to have their card?"

The guy stretches his legs and sticks both hands in his jeans' pockets. The girl searches inside her angular purse.

"I love your bag." I interject.

"Oh, thank you. Sullivan gave it to me for our third-month anniversary."

Dear oh dear, I think, losing all respect for them both. My private guessing game is utterly spoiled. Third-month anniversary! Children! Sullivan takes the room key from its paper holder that has all the details of the hotel and holds it out to me.

"Sorry, that's the best I can do."

"Thanks a lot! You sure you don't need it?"

"Nah, that's fine."

My neighbours have gone and the restaurant crowd is getting sparse. I ask the waiter for a pen and cross out 604, the neighbours' room number. Those three digits will not play a part in my plan.

I have had four dishes comprising the most exquisite flavours; all made by the chef himself, as I requested. I am watching him now place very thin streaks of meat, origin mysterious, onto a bed of something that looks like green jelly, the same dark colour as seaweed. He takes a fresh bottle of champagne from the fridge and pops it open, pours a minuscule amount in a glass, exactly up to one of the numbered lines and pours it over the green jelly. He takes the plate with both hands, walks around the glass counter and places it in front of me.

"It's lovely to see you here," he says, and I still

wonder if he has been ignoring me all night. "This is the surprise of the night. Enjoy your dessert."

"With meat?" I ask, before he can escape.

"But is it meat?" he says with a smirk. "You'll have to find out."

He goes back to his command centre, and those streaks in my plate are definitely not meat. The jelly is quite certainly a mix of green tea and a pinch of cinnamon. The round shapes at the top, although a crimson colour, must be dark chocolate truffles.

"Chef!" I call out to him as his back is to me. He turns hurriedly and comes forward, puts his hands on the ledges of the glass counter.

"Yes? How did you like your dessert?"

"Orgasmic."

"Glad to hear that, especially your colourful description."

"You're the man who inspires my language. That plate was like a painting."

"Thank you. Always a pleasure to serve you."

"Long day?"

"Indeed. But not much longer to call it a night."

"I'm going to have a drink here," and I slide the card towards him. "Why don't you come join me when you're finished?"

He smiles a cheeky smile and makes a gesture with his head that could mean anything. "See you later," he says as he turns his attention back to work.

A man of about sixty, in a black coat that nearly touches his boots and a top hat at least one size too small, holds open the door to The Blue Fin and utters a discrete welcome. The lobby is light, but I am more interested in the darkness to the left. Before I move inside the bar, I walk to the reception and ask for a room for the night. After going through the formalities I walk to the bar and take a stool. A bartender, probably a full-time student, places the menu in front of me and smiles. He has gorgeous dark eyes, with lashes so long they nearly touch his glasses.

"I don't need that. Can I have a bottle of Merlot?"

"Of course. Would you like to choose which variety?" He asks in a gentle voice that matches those innocent eyes. How I wish I could corrupt him. Maybe I should just tease him a little.

"Why don't you do the choosing for me, sweetie?"

I can't see him blush, but his voice certainly does and his eyes immediately look down, his smile gets wider and he rushes off to pick my bottle.

I haven't finished my first glass when I feel a hand lightly rest on the small of my back.

I cock an eyebrow over my shoulder and smile slowly. "You came."

He smiles in response and folds himself elegantly onto the seat next to mine. The young waiter tops up my drink and pours him one.

"Cheers," I say and our glasses touch and shriek a tiny clink. "Not traumatised by the fish attack, are we?"

He laughs a throaty laugh, softer than the bright public one for the benefit of his kitchen.

"I thought you, of all people, would know that my skin is much thicker. Traumatising me requires serious skill," he says, suddenly earnest.

"Mmmm," I murmur, "I'm sure it does. Look at him!" I suggest, indicating with an arched eyebrow the floppy haired barman, who has been eyeing us with failed discretion. "I think he likes me."

"He's what? Twenty? Looking for a Toy Boy?"

"And your point?" I pretend to pout. "All men need an older woman in their education. Wouldn't you agree? Or have you forgotten your own trajectory in that regard?"

"I was hoping you wouldn't recall that in this situation, but your memory is as infuriatingly crystalline as ever!"

"Come on, tell me the story again. I believe I may have mislaid some of the more delightful details."

"I think that's unlikely, if you've heard it once you've heard it a thousand times."

"I know. But humour me. A lady's privilege!"

"OK, OK." He relents. "I was twenty-one. My parents had just got divorced. I didn't mind the divorce, but I hated the deception. All my life they'd behaved as if they were teenage lovers. But it was a lie and I couldn't handle it. I dropped out of my business course at University. I packed a rucksack, emptied my bank account, (though it hardly had enough for my airfare in it). I got myself to Osaka Airport and the first available flight turned out to be to Helsinki. I took it without knowing anything about the city."

"Yes I remember. And then what did you do next?"

"Well as soon as I took my seat and we'd got into the air I asked the flight attendant for pen and paper and started jotting down possibilities, what I thought I might be good at, things that would possibly earn me a living till I figured things out. The paper was half full when the woman sitting beside me commented on it. She said she wished she could read my beautiful handwriting, and that the Japanese alphabet baffled and bemused her."

"One can tell rather a lot about a man by the way he handles a pen. And what did she look like?"

"Expensive, is how she looked. Enfolded in layers of beige cashmere and silk, all the variations of golden in a perfect Napoleon. That perfectly graduated caramel hair. She smelled like soap and citrus and baby powder and flowers. Chanel No.19, as I later discovered."

"What a romantic description chef, you're surpassing yourself. Go on."

"She talked for a rather long time, mostly about Japan and how much she loved it. She said she travelled there for inspiration at least once a year. I liked the charm in her voice and how she glowed when she talked about the mundane, everyday things that I took for granted, never thought twice about. She asked me what my story was and what was taking me to Helsinki, a girlfriend, studies, what? 'I am travelling to forget,' I said. 'Forget what?' she asked. 'A lot,' I replied and told her about my parents. I told her that I couldn't even locate Finland on a map and I was on this flight because it was the first out of Osaka. She asked about my plans and I told her I had none. She asked where I was going to sleep that night and I replied I needed to find a hostel. 'Are you any good in the kitchen?' she asked, which I found a bizarre question at the time. I said I had worked in McDonald's in Kyoto for six months and I sometimes cooked my meals before I dropped out of university. 'Fantastic!' She put a hand on my arm, and wrapped her fingers around it with determination, then she said: 'You're hired.' Puzzled and excited, I asked what she meant. 'I mean, you are going to come and work in my restaurant and with that job there will be accommodation, so you can set aside your hostel idea.' I asked her if she was serious. Of course she was. I took her hand with both my hands and shook it hard and repeatedly bowed (as well as I could from sitting position, as the seatbelt light was on) to show my gratitude and she laughed hysterically, waking a few people and causing a flight attendant to rush over and ask if everything was OK. I reassured him in my broken English that everything was in fact more than wonderful. He left us with a confused look. But I've run on for far too long already."

"Don't you dare stop now."

"I'm afraid I must draw a veil over some of the details. A gentleman doesn't kiss and tell. Long story short, the woman who gave me a job and jumpstarted my career was also my first serious lover, although she was only a couple of years younger than my mother. I spent six years of my life with her."

"That's cheating," I objected. "You're missing out all the exciting parts."

"I think my dear, that you are quite capable of providing a great deal of excitement yourself without leaving the present."

"Well in that case..." I hand him one of the room cards. "See you in Room 333. Go now." I make a gesture of benign dismissal. More of a benediction.

"Yes, my lady. Thank you for the wine, which was of a surpassing flavour rarely tasted in these lands." He gives a courtly bow.

"I can tell you one thing, you've come a long way when it comes to your linguistic skills. Must be the result of your wife's brilliance."

"Well my lovely wife," he leans towards my ear, "that is undoubtedly true. But it takes some time to adjust to your dazzle. Take care not to let your brilliance overwhelm lesser mortals. They might fry like Sisyphus." He laughs softly, sending a warm frisson over my body.

As he walks towards the lifts, I divert my attention to Sisyphus behind the bar. The bar is much quieter now and he is trying to look busy. But how can he resist my eyes? He comes to me, with a goofy smile.

"Can I get you anything else, madam?"

"Of course, you can, my darling." I stretch my open hand towards him, sending him immediately somersaulting out of his comfort zone, but all he can do is put his hand in mine. I press his hand gently in mine. "You can first tell me your name."

"Solomon."

"Solomon! Your hand is too soft for a king. And your eyes too innocent." Perhaps not enough grit for Sisyphus. Aloud, "Sampson perhaps."

He looks deeply abashed. Hmm. He must be up on his classics. I let his fingers slip. "I'll tell you what you can get me, sweet Solomon. Another bottle of

Merlot, in Room 333."

"Of course, madam. I'll send it up straight away."

"No, no, no. No sending, my dear. You shall bring it yourself. And we will need three glasses."

"I work in the bar. I am not allowed to leave it."

"Then you will do it right after you finish work. Shouldn't be too long now." I wink at him, as if he needs any more discomfort.

"I could lose my job for that kind of thing, madam."

"First of all, stop 'madam-ing' me. Call me Elana. And surely you can't possibly be chastised for meeting the service requirements of a guest?" I smile, just a little wickedly. He meets my eyes. I see a flash of the man he might become. "Furthermore, fortune favours the brave. Courage young man, I look forward to seeing you shortly."

As I walk out of the bar towards the lifts, I can feel his stare tracing over my body, measuring me up and down. I thank God that even after several glasses of wine I've never struggled to walk in four-inch heels (pain bedamned) and sashay a little for his benefit.

I take the lift to the third floor and step over the threshold, straight out of my shoes. I walk slowly into the room and wonder if the boy Solomon will join us. I do hope so. A new ingredient in a classic pairing is always welcome. It has done wonders for my marriage of ten years.

Korean appliances were the first of the country's products to woo Iranians. Washing machines, fridges and freezers filled stores in cities big and small across the country in the nineties. Alongside these white goods, televisions and cassette players found their way into Iranian homes. In the years after the war people gradually became wealthier as the economy grew, so then came the Korean dishwashers and microwave ovens, partly because of the beauty of the product design, compared to the ugly Iranian versions. Computers, mobile phones and laptops followed closely behind.

State TV – the only TV – began broadcasting a series from Korea in the mid-noughties. *Jewel of the Palace*, the story of a poor girl who was being trained to be a royal chef, became so popular that Iran sent a reporter to interview Dae Jang Kum, the heroine of the story. The programme attracted over seven million viewers. No wonder her photographs were on the cover of so many magazines, partly thanks to the absence of copyright laws in the country.

When I was a university student, I met a Korean journalist at a party. He was amazed by how much alcohol was consumed in parties in a country that was supposed to be a "dry land". I proudly invited him to come and see my friend Navid's private brewery. He then wrote a feature about it in a weekly in Seoul and sent me a copy. It was uncanny to see a photograph of the little shed as the main picture of his article. He'd translated the headline and written in green ink below the Korean script, "Hidden Pleasures of a Theocratic Land, by Dong Yup Park". There were other pictures. He took a photo of people dancing to DJ Tiesto at the party. But aware of the risks that might threaten his models, he decreased the shutter speed to a point where the photograph turned into a trance-like whizz of colour and haze.

Another fashionable TV series showed the glories of knighthood in ancient Korea, *the Legend of Ju Mong*. I had the head start on everyone this time. I managed the accounts of a major Korean electronics company. I phoned Dong and asked him about the actor who played the lead role in the series. He was surprised to hear how popular the celebrity was among Iranians and said he would be happy to find him for me. The next morning I received an email from him with contact details of Yeoun Ju Lee, the actor's agent who, luckily, *did* speak English.

A woman with a strong American accent answered my call. When I asked to speak to Ms Ju Lee, she said, "Speaking." That was a good sign. My Korean client was delighted to hear my pitch and happy to fund the touring campaign. Then I got the Islamic Republic of Iran Broadcasting involved without giving them the smallest of concessions, teasing the hell out of their Asian fetish. I told them it was our show but we were prepared to work with them if they wanted. A month later we hosted a group of eleven Koreans who toured the country. The publicity was massive; the electronics firm couldn't have dreamt of it. They flew in one of their senior managers to give a speech at the main reception and say how proud he was to see the art of his country celebrated in Iran.

I was a second-year student at university when I started that first job, which went on to be my only job. I complained to my friends that I didn't enjoy my subject; neither did I cherish the thought of becoming a chemical engineer in a few years time. They reminded me that the title 'Engineer' before any name added bucketloads of prestige to it in Iran. They were right, but that was not my sole purpose in life.

Pedram was in my class and I'd got him started on the joys of hiking. We'd formed a group that went for walks on the trails around Tehran almost every week. One day he showed me a job advert for a respected advertising agency. Although I joked about what use they would have for chemistry students, he insisted that we should apply. We went through three rounds of interviews and were both accepted as junior account executives. Pedram left the company after less than a year, whining about how it was too much trouble juggling studies and work, but I stayed on. Work comprised assisting the account managers on different projects, attending marketing promotions and preparing presentations. Later on, as my career progressed, I was myself promoted to be an account manager and assigned my own client.

If you are staying in Esteghlal Hotel in a north-facing room on the thirteenth floor, you are on an elite list of the extremely fortunate. Particularly if it is April and the mountains you can see from those huge windows are still covered in snow. If you wake up early enough, when the sunbeams are still struggling to climb all the way from the back of the Alborz wall of mountains, you'll be able to see blue sky untainted with pollution. You can open the window and breathe in the fresh oxygen that you know has touched the snow. You can see the Parkway Bridge just by the foot of the hotel and all the early commuters in cars, on buses, in taxis or on their motorbikes. And if you turn your head forty-five degrees to the right, you'll be able to see the glorious Mount Damavand in a distance.

I put my arm round the bare waist of Yeoun Ju Lee and told her all about Damavand, the country's highest mountain. I told her there was a war in ancient times between Iran and our westerly neighbour Turan, that Iranian forces were pushed back and were close to defeat, so there were negotiations to end the war. It was agreed that an archer would determine the fate of Iran's border. Arash, a great archer in the king's service, was given a legendary bow and arrow by his lord, and asked to carry out the task. Arash knew that in spite of the great tools he had been given, he would surely die after shooting from the peak of Mount Damavand, for it would require all of his life force to achieve the feat, but he was willing, for he loved his king and his homeland.

"Arash let fly his arrow from the great bow, and fell dead, but his arrow travelled from the morning till the evening and landed on a walnut tree by the River Jayhun, and there the border was set." I concluded, grazing her shoulder with my lips.

"There's something in the air of your mountains," Yeoun Ju said, "or perhaps in the tale you tell. It makes me feel alive."

She arched her back and her legs, tossing and turning her body in my embrace. How could I resist? It hadn't taken us long to fall into bed together; only two days. On arrival she was suffering wickedly from jet lag; the entire Korean squad had. From noon of the second day I'd had a perpetual semi in expectation of what the evening would bring. There was something in her gaze that assured me she reciprocated my desire. I couldn't be sure at that stage, but I loved the tease.

The tour went to Tabriz, Isfahan, Shiraz and even the holy city of Mashhad. We fucked in every city and each time with the urgency and awareness of temporary lovers. Knowing that made us even more insatiable. We wanted more.

Yeoun Ju Lee was flying to China in the afternoon to negotiate a deal for the celebrity who had returned to Seoul a night earlier. I'd booked the day off to come to terms with the fact that the surreal period was almost over. I needed half a day on my own, or perhaps a meet up with Navid in his shop or Crazy Beans, to get back to reality.

"It'll never be the same again," I said.

"What?" Ju Lee replied.

"The way I see Koreans."

"Interesting. Tell me about it."

She slipped the robe over her lovely shoulders.

"You guys look like you're good at being static."

"You guys look like you spend half of your time in mosques, praying to Allah, and the other half loitering around, doing nothing."

"I still can't believe you came four times in a row."

"I still can't believe how good you are with your tongue. I thought it'd be unthinkable, not just that, the whole thing."

"You were amazing."

"You were much better than expected."

"But–"

"Let's stop it, shall we?"

"Absolutely."

I sat still on the bed, naked, and watched her pack. The smell of freshly-brewed coffee was mixed with her body lotion and the scent of jasmine curling from a vase on the side table. From the sound of it, the street was choking with the morning rush hour and I was choking with longing. She took the robe off, folded it and forced it into her suitcase that had a blue ribbon tied to its handle.

"You're really nicking the robe, Yeoun Ju Lee?"

"Yes, of course, I like it. But why do you use my full name?" She uttered the sentence as she walked to me and knelt inside my legs, swaying her body upwards against mine.

"I like the sound of it."

"And I like how you sound when you fuck me. Will you let me hear you one last time, Mr Hekmat?"

"Are you serious?"

"Why do you think I served you a double espresso for breakfast?"

"I just thought you were being devastatingly chic. But devastatingly chic and devious is even better!"

"You can rest all through the rush hour," she giggled.

"One last time, then."

White

If you stand close enough, it looks like a bucket of light splashed over the canvas. You take a few steps back and a room flooded with the reflection of the Bosphorus is born. White walls, like linen washed and hung to dry in the sun, swirl around, crisp and imperfect.

The paintings, some as big as the windowpanes, others just a fraction of the size, mostly chosen with reasonable curatorial taste, almost create the illusion of beauty. But she is not convinced. Didn't anybody think before polluting this perfect pure space with 'art'? She closes her eyes and imagines all the artworks gone, the room decluttered, the windows open, the sea breeze free to come in from any direction. She circumnavigates the room slowly, twirling the curls that fall over her ears in one finger.

There is a song in her head. She pauses and then walks to the window, squeezing her brain to remember what music it is trying to escape from inside her. She puts her palms on the glass and gets as close as earthly possible to it and squints to see further than possible, trying to detect the Maiden Tower across the water. She isn't entirely sure if it is the haze that prevents her or her eyesight, maybe it is too far for any normal eye to see that far. But is it really far? She closes her eyes again and sees the stone building and its irregular dome, its erected mast and the red flag.

The wild breeze is kept safely locked out. She walks around the room and inspects any area of the wall that is not covered with art. She doesn't completely ignore the paintings, but looks at them with suspicion, the kind of suspicion that you reserve for your mother's best friend whom you suspect of having an affair with your dad. But when she comes face to face with a particular artwork, she surprises herself by feeling not the smallest trace of suspicion or discomfort or even unease. It's just that the walls are so much more interesting. She has trouble articulating this thought to herself.

Imagine you are at the seaside and you collect pebbles of all sizes and colours. You put them all together on sand and create the shape of a body, of course not a perfect form; it is a figure in all its imperfect, unique splendour. If you were to pull out a white sheet of paper, dampened to softness, and run it over the pebbles, using your fingers to emboss the shape of each one in the paper the result would be an unadulterated interpretation of shape. White, textured, moulded. Raw, and yet pure. She smiles.

Involuntarily, she plays with her toes, still encased in her shoes, as if they are buried in sand. The smell of the sea plays in her nostrils and she suddenly feels a breeze twisting round her legs. She turns around in pleasant surprise to investigate, which window has been opened and who has let such a force of freedom loose in the church-like gallery. The windows are still shut. A woman has walked past her, at a pace too brisk for the context of a museum of modern art. She follows the woman's steps with her eyes and moves her head up slowly, from the tan, ankle-length boots to the tight black jeans, the narrow camel belt, the white, white, white shirt. The mystery woman stops across from her and looks, as Tania did, out the window. Tania likes her cropped, elfish blond hair and the simple elegance with which she carries herself.

She feels the blood run fast to her face when the source of her interest turns around to continue her visit. Tania hastily turns back to the wall and stares fixedly at the white artwork. A drum roll is beginning inside her chest and she feels as if she has been transported in time back to elementary school, when she had been naughty and been forced to wait outside the classroom to be punished. There is a strange pleasure in tasting this experience, this tense memory at the edge of her consciousness chiming with a present moment. An element of fear combined with not knowing. She finds herself going up and down on her toes, shifted into a simpler, readier self: restless.

As she turns her head around, carefully, slowly, she sees the blonde already at the far end of the room, open the sliding glass door and enter the café, speak to the waiter, point at the terrace outside and go straight to the other sliding door at the other end. She follows in her footsteps, into the café and out again to the terrace that sits quietly overlooking the strait. She leaves one table vacant in between but sits at an angle that gives her a direct view of the breeze-maker.

It is now the empty terrace, the two of them, their Turkish coffees – one *orta*, half sugar, and one black, the occasional shriek of the seagulls and generous amounts of sea breeze.

The blonde turns her head to the left and without hesitation says: "why did you sit that far?"

Blood floods her face again and she finds it impossible to respond. She smiles deeper into her flush. She is a teenager again. She manages to look the blonde in the eye, the meeting of their eyes is like a physical touch. She is fully alive now, thrumming.

"Well, the mountain will move if you won't," says the blonde, smiling. She stands, takes her cup and relocates to the seat beside Tania. She strokes Tania's hand, stretched out on the table. What has she got in those fingers? Tania catches her breath as the touch ignites desire. She closes her eyes and lets the electricity of those fingers running over her hand tantalise her. She imagines the two of them standing alone by the sea, without the ugly presence of waiters and customers and seagulls and bloody art galleries. She imagines the stylish garb of the blonde gone and her body shining. She quivers and holds her hand tight. 'I want you and there is nothing else that I want more.' She makes the thought an intention, it quivers in the air. The blonde watches her enjoy the moment. She squeezes her hand, too.

A week has passed and she is back on the terrace, stalking the ferries that swim across the narrow passage that separates Asia from Europe. She is on the European side, but how she longs for her Europe, how restless is she, how completely lost. Why didn't she ask her to stay?

First published in the Erotic Review Magazine.

I followed her down Berkeley Street as she walked under patched-up, grey, autumn clouds, taking long steps that hid her speed. The city and its inhabitants saw a young woman sporting a crimson handbag; her lips the same deep colour. They saw her soft, brown hair playfully swirling and jumping over that beige dress. I saw more: The shampoo that was responsible for the gloss of her hair, the moisturiser that had hints of lavender in it, the bra that had nothing to do with the perkiness of her breasts, the two puffs of Revlon Charlie on each side of the neck, the left earring missing the hinge. Yet I was as unknown to her as anybody else on that road.

She turned left onto Piccadilly and continued at the same pace to the Royal Academy. She sat at a table in the outdoor café. I walked past and went straight into the gift shop and bought a postcard.

When I returned, she had been served mint tea in a glass pot. She had already eaten half the tuna and cucumber sandwich that she had made in the morning: how patiently she had worked the knife, spreading butter over the brown bread.

After four weeks of watching every move she made, and the day had come to make contact. I waited for her to finish her lunch and go inside. I followed after a few minutes. I watched her absorb the paintings, moving from one to the next with hesitation, as if something was yet to be explored before the next chapter began. Her gaze lingered but the legs moved forth.

When the moment was right, as she was trying to cut loose her gaze from one artwork and move to the next, I ever so casually placed my arm where it could bump into hers, and, as it did, I let the records in my hand fly and fall, all three of them. Each touched the floor with its own specific sound, depending on the material of the jacket.

"My, oh my! I'm so sorry. Look what I've done!" she said, hurriedly trying to collect the vinyl.

I crouched with her, pretending to do the same thing and telling her it was no big deal. "You must have been completely absorbed in the art," I said.

"How did you get this?" She was holding tight to *The Name of The Game*. She looked at it in amazement and exchanged a glance or two with me.

She had bit the bait. The first stage of the plan had worked. And even better, she'd already ignored my stupid question about how intently she was looking at the paintings and the whole thing about flying vinyl was no longer the focus of conversation.

"That! Erm, a mate works in the studio of the music label. He dumps a taster or two on me every now and then."

"But this will only be released in a month, right?"

"Quite possibly." I held her arm gently and raised her to standing. "Do you want it?"

"What? Are you serious?"

"If you like the music, you should have it. I barely know the band."

"I love ABBA. But this is really embarrassing. I first knock you out and then take your vinyl away."

"Not at all. You didn't quite knock me out."

We walked around the gallery and talked. She said how much she loved art and that, although it was her job to look at art and to appreciate it, there was something much deeper than that. It was the only reason life was worth living. How could one describe how profound the curves are on a Moore wooden sculpture? She asked in all seriousness. Was there any better way of showing horror than in Goya's black paintings?

I knew everything about her work already, about her life spinning around art, her days spent with painted canvases and pretty sculptures, but the way she spoke about it, her sheer enthusiasm, her zest, her passionate eyes, shook me. How could one be so innocent, so unrelentingly full of life?

"Let me invite you to lunch this Friday to thank you for this." She said with a bright smile, as if it was natural to do it in those days.

"As much as I would like to accept your kind offer, I'm afraid I'll be abroad. These days I get to walk in Mayfair only once every couple of months."

"Oh, where are you going?"

"I have some business in Sardinia, will be there for at least a couple of weeks."

"You can't be serious!"

I pretended to be taken aback: "I am very serious."

"No, I mean, I am going to Cagliari the Wednesday after."

"Ah, what a coincidence! Antico Caffè, then. They do the best seafood salad imaginable."

A coincidence constructed by me, planned and trimmed and made to measure. She told me where she'd be staying, wrote my number in a tiny leather-bound notebook that she produced by digging a hand in her purse, and promised she'd call me as soon as she got to her hotel. She had gone, but her scent lingered on. I walked around the Academy aimlessly for another hour or so. I don't recall if

I looked at any paintings. I walked and walked and walked. The thought of what was in store was hard to bear. I had been on the job for years and no project, not a single one, had made me feel like this before. Tingled and tickled inside when on surveillance. At the end of the day, this was my job. I got it done and moved on each time.

It was the beginning of October, when despite the 28-degree days the Sardo people refused to go to the beach, sell sunscreen or even acknowledge that it was summer.

I'd arranged to meet her at the sea front, have a walk and then go for lunch. The breeze made the midday heat more tolerable and painted waves in the air with her hair. We joked about the locals already wearing jumpers. We walked around the marina and watched the sea patiently have its way with the boats. We went uphill towards the café, but I wanted to show her the staggering views from Piazza Martiri D'Italia. Undermined by an empty stomach, every step made for a challenging climb. It was all worth it once we got there. The palms danced against a background of the marina and miles and miles of azure Mediterranean Sea. I took her gently by the hand and twirled her softly, her long form echoing the trees above our heads. She laughed out loud and swirled and swirled and swirled.

“That’s where we will eat,” I pointed to the building at the square below the building while my other arm wrapped around her and rested on her belly. “It’s the oldest restaurant in town.”

What would it be like to have a life like this? In a frenzy of imagination I put her and I in a life shared, a together life, a country house in Sardinia or Sussex, a normal way of living, a nine-to-five job, an office salary, kids, lazy weekends.

“I would never have guessed you had such a passion for food!” She teased. “You must be getting excited; your heart’s beating really fast.” I wished she was right, that it was all that simple, that animalistic, that human. Food and sex. None of it was.

Lunch was delicious, I guess. She said she wanted a different job, that loving art and selling it were two different things. I wished I could tell her I wanted a different job, too. What would she think of me if she knew what I did? What if she knew the bubble we were in was meticulously created with lies?

The more she talked about her job, the more I was filled with doubt. It was a big mistake to get involved, to talk to her, to listen to her. I should have done my job and left. Why her? She owned a small gallery, looked at pretty things and put a price on them. I didn’t understand, but I was certain the reason behind the assignment was strong. My employers would not pay me to do a job without strong rationale behind it, I was sure of that. There must have been something else. The arts, the gallery, must have all been a mere distraction.

"There's no point in coming to Sardinia if you don't get to see Piscinas." I told her.

"What is it?"

"The most beautiful beach with the most exquisite sand dunes. You think the West Indies, the Maldives or The Keys are beautiful, but there is only one Piscinas in the world and it's in a league of its own."

"Do you work for the Sardinian tourist board? You're selling this really well."

"Not at all. I appreciate beauty and when I see something extraordinary I like to share it."

"I wish I could see it."

"What's stopping you?"

"I'm flying back to London tomorrow."

"How about changing your flight and staying the weekend?"

"I don't think I can change this one."

"Say you want to stay and I'll take care of your ticket."

"I do, but how?"

Without answering her, I walked to the bar and asked if I could use the telephone. I dialled a number just short of a digit and pretended talking to someone about her flight, gave her name and said I'd pick up the ticket later.

"That's that," I told her as I sat down and put my serviette back on my lap.

"It's done?"

"Yes. This is a small place. As long as you know the right people, nothing is impossible."

"I'd better go shopping for a bikini."

"That'll be hard work. Don't even bother with sun cream, they've stopped selling it. The Sardinian summer is gone."

Morning sunshine poured on the smooth tarmac like honey. The road from Cagliari was wide and open, with the occasional car driving past the white convertible I was driving. She sat with a sleepy smile and listened to the radio, Italian music and intermittent commentary.

"Do you speak Italian?" I asked.

"No, but I like the sound of it."

"It rolls easily."

"Don't you find it difficult to drive on the wrong side of the road?"

"Right or wrong? The entire philosophical notion is a fallacy. There is no such thing as right or wrong. It is how you see things, how you put them in the context."

"You sound very immoral – and very serious too," she touched my knee with two fingers and slid them all the way up over my thigh. I looked back at her and smiled.

"Morality is overrated."

We drove north all the way to Sanluri and then turned west, where the road became narrower and the trees came closer to the edge. Only a few more minutes of driving and we were already beginning to crawl up the mountains. We drove past some malnourished-looking goats before the road began winding over the next few mountains from Guspini onwards. The tarmac came to an end by an old mine and the Costa Verde began to show its charm. Soon the sand dunes appeared and before we knew it, we had Piscinas and its wild beach pretty much to ourselves. There were only three caravans and a few cars parked, and a kiosk was open for beer and snacks.

She jumped out of the car without opening the door. In a quick move she freed herself from the dress she was wearing and threw it on the back seat.

"Woohoo, this is more like it! Let's go get wet."

She ran to the sea over the sand and I stood there watching her skin glow under the sunshine. My hand was still on the door handle, but I couldn't stop looking at her childlike excitement. She was already splashing in the Mediterranean.

"Come on, why are you stuck there?" she shouted.

I spread the towel on the beach and sat on it, mesmerised by the view of her dancing with the melting waves. She wanted me to join her, but I'd been dreading the moment for days. She came out splashing the seawater at me and jumped on me. We wrestled and I let her win, defeat me, keep me under her motionless. I wished fervently she could keep me there. But she kissed me and said I should take a dip into the sea.

I stood up but couldn't feel my limbs; they were numb all over. I dragged myself towards the sea, my heart beating so fast and so hard I imagined every bit of my body having a small heart of its own, all beating relentlessly. She took my hand and tried to make me join her in the speed and enthusiasm.

"Come on, what's the matter with you?"

I cooked up a fake smile and said I was fine. When the water touched my toes, an electric shock went through my spine. What was wrong with me? Why had I allowed myself to get involved with a project this much? Ridiculous. Unacceptable. The change of mood was staggering. I took her hand and pulled her in.

"Swim with me," I told her.

That made her laugh. "That's much better. Are we racing then?" And she swam into the horizon.

I followed her and encouraged her to carry on. We went so far that the kiosk looked as small as a match-box. I drew her near and kissed her lips and gazed at her unsuspecting eyes. I touched her ears with my fingers and let my hands slide down and rest on her shoulders. I pushed her under water. She must have thought it was another game, like the wrestling on the sand, and didn't resist much. After a few seconds she began jerking her body and grabbing at my arms and shoulders. She even managed to nearly get her head above the water; she came close enough that I saw the fear and confusion in her eyes. Was it fear or disbelief? I couldn't tell then and I cannot tell now.

I stayed there and kept her close long after she'd ceased to move, running my fingers over her back and arms. I finally let go of the body and swam back to the shore. I shook the sand off the towel, folded it neatly and walked back to the car, avoiding the kiosk.

Back in Cagliari, I dragged myself into a bar with plastic chairs set outside in the shade of an Acacia tree. I ordered a bottle of wine in my flaky Italian and asked if they sold cigarettes. The waiter, who must have been around my age, smiled and asked for *un momento*, gesturing with his raised index finger. He took out his own packet and offered me one. I took it, but was embarrassed to find my hand was shaking. He lit a match for me and went straight back into the shop.

It was only after a couple of glasses of wine that my heartbeat started to drop back to normal. There is a first for everything: a shaking hand, a racing heart, a head full of doubt.

The waiter pulled up a chair and joined me. He lit two cigarettes and offered me one. Marcello was the name, he said as he shook my hand.

"Don't worry, mate. You say mate for friend in England, no? What is it that bother you now you will forget tomorrow. Trust me. Time is...*come l'oceano* you understand? It washes away all the things."

His words made my stomach, slowly relaxing, tighten again. Too apt by half.

"I wish I could believe that. I doubt time is a strong enough remedy for this one."

"Listen, things look one thing but are one thing else. Like you have this expression, don't only look at a book's jacket."

"Don't judge a book by its cover."

"Yes, that. See, this way: I serve you wine. You call me barman. *Corretto*?"

"Yes, *corretto*."

"Is barman the only thing I am?"

He turned around and shouted in Italian to a boy who was cleaning the floor, asking him to bring *il libro*. The boy rolled his eyes, but obliged.

"This is my poems."

It wasn't a notebook of scribbles, but a fully bound and catalogued volume, with a publisher's imprint.

"Look."

"What are you trying to say?"

"*Allora*. Keep the book. We all have many pages. Don't worry. You will be out of this mood. I get back to work now, okay?"

What did I know about poetry, I thought. I had more in common with the kitchen boy, cleaning up messes. I got an assignment, got it done, got paid. What did I know about anything at all? Did I know the reason behind any of my assignments? Did I ever question any of it? Such thoughts are luxuries: luxuries that weaken the will.

I had already wasted enough time and needed to move on to the next job. Maybe the best thing was calling my employers and checking in. Next.

First published in Stories from around the World, an anthology by THotel Cagliari.